A Wrong Turn
on the
Search for a
Signing

L.B. Robbins

Copyright © 2021 by L.B. Robbins

All rights reserved. No part of this publication may be reproduced, distributed, or transmitted in any form or by any means, including photocopying, recording, or other electronic or mechanical methods, without the prior written permission of the publisher, except in the case brief quotations embodied in critical reviews and other noncommercial uses permitted by copyright law.

ISBN: 978-1-954341-39-5 (Paperback)

The views expressed in this book are solely those of the author and do not necessarily reflect the views of the publisher, and the publisher hereby disclaims any responsibility for them.

Writers' Branding
1800-608-6550
www.writersbranding.com
orders@writersbranding.com

Contents

Introduction
Chapter 1: Off to The Book Signing — 3
Chapter 2: At the Taj — 7
Chapter 3: At another overnight party — 12
Chapter 4: Off we go into the wild blue yonder — 16
Chapter 5: At the signing — 20
Chapter 6: Deep in the night — 25
Chapter 7: On the road again — 27
Chapter 8: At the bus terminal — 30
Chapter 9: Along the Inter Coastal — 33
Chapter 10: Angellica at the breakfast club — 36
Chapter 11: The trail picks up steam — 40
Chapter 12: A new dimension for Angellica — 42
Chapter 13: The story unfolds in the car — 47
Chapter 14: A strange turn of events — 50
Chapter 15: Inside the Hospital — 54
Chapter 16: Back at the Treetops — 56
Chapter 17: Home at last — 61

INTRODUCTION

The drab little train chugged faithfully along the monotonous landscape of tired leaves and brush. Margaret followed it intently with her usual sad eyes, absentmindedly reviewing recent months since her remarkably uneventful graduation.

Seeing the uniformed procession of blue and white tassels marching silently to their destination, it was just another unremarkable proof of her unsuccessful social life. No fond family in the small bleachers or tight knot of friends clapping her enthusiastically onward. Only memories of annoying meetings with advisors and lonely weekend evenings in the dorm persisted in her mind.

She'd always been a loner. Lack of funds in later years had seen to that, that and a persistent look of moderate facial features and dull hair and eyes had sealed her fate in the dormitory over the past four years. Only a sharp mind and literary zeal set her apart from the maddening crowd at the small Midwest college. If it hadn't been for scholarships, no graduation would have been possible.

The perfect novelist, although as yet unknown, her mind was now centered on her most recent fantasy being plotted and her unexpected good luck at snatching employment with her favorite author.

L.B. Robbins

Unbelievably she had been chosen from a lucky group of contestants to become assistant to one of the most successful authors of this generation, HC Hemmings.

The train pulled into the station where she hoped to be met by staff to meet this highly celebrated heroin of hers. Next it would be on to an unexpected vacation at a lakefront lodge. Oh yes, it had all been worth it!

CHAPTER ONE

Off to The Book Signing

The beautiful Town Car was smoothly headed toward Sea Isle City. Every possible gear in its machinery hummed out the first class engineering involved in the development of this, Angellica Peterson's new acquisition. It was out for a first class trial run to Mullica Hill near Philadelphia to put its pistons to the test, if that was what they were called. They were turning noiselessly, she was pretty sure.

Angie had had an unexpected inheritance, and she celebrated in the best way she knew she'd purchased a new car. The old Ford just couldn't make it these days. Now in the car of her dreams, she made the rounds of the markets on the other side of the bridge and was in possession of a horde of down home in her front seat. "Guess I drove the kinks out of her, and got rid of the new car smell", she thought.

Soon she'd be enjoying the fruits of her days outing in her small kitchen at home. Now she'd just bask in the smells of her purchases and enjoy the changing leaves of the trees as she drove along route 77, through the most beautiful countryside of south Jersey, the last of the small truck farms in the state.

As she spotted her small lane and drove up the rather long driveway leading to her back porch, she had that usual feeling of proud ownership. Looking at the smartly trimmed shrubs and well kept lawn, Angie kept the same lawn standards her husband and she both had had for twenty years.

She could hear the phone ringing before she entered the back door. They'll call back if they need me. She struggled with her bags, and once again was reminded of how lonely it was without the helping hands of her beloved husband. He would have run ahead and answered the phone, carrying half of these valued purchases, which they would have enjoyed together.

The ringing stopped just as she was about to answer.

"Hi, it's Holly" said a familiar voice.

Angie quickly grabbed the call before it could be lost and gladly responded.

This was a very old friend of hers, a voice of the past, HC Hemmings who'd gone on to become a pretty well known author. She was one of her more successful sorority sisters, with her own faithful following of readers. She was one of them.

"I'm in town for a book signing at the Taj Mahal and I hope you can come on Saturday" was her request.

"Sure, I'd love to see you again. It's been such a long time!" and we went on to discuss several of the friends we had together, and the few small time scandals they'd been up to so far.

"Oh, Angie, it's so good to hear your voice. Why don't we meet for dinner Friday evening and get to trash some of our old friends together. I'm here in town all alone and you know me and being alone on a Friday evening.

She was alluding to the fact that, in our day, she was one of the most popular in our set of friends, and was never alone in the dorms weekends. So many of us usually were in this sorry state. Rob and I were dating, but he was a serious student in a masters program. I spent much of the time alone, it was so much better for our grades. I had assumed that explained in

A Wrong Turn of the Search for a Signing

the best light his preoccupation with his studies. Fortunately it turned out to be true.

What will I wear, as I sat down in my small living room. This was my first thought. I had only one "success" outfit, so that was not the problem. Would Holly be impressed?

Probably not, I thought.

She was the only I knew who'd gone on to make it big in the fast line, which was what I called it. None of us were really surprised. It seemed that everything Holly touched turned to gold. She had a happy marriage, lived in several of her beautiful homes on both coasts and wanted for nothing. A great career as an author only seemed natural to me. As for Holly, she could capture a mood on paper like no one else I knew.

It was no surprise that she was here in town at the Taj Majal for a book signing. I sighed with just a twinge of jealousy.

So it really wasn't a case of what to wear.

I only had one "almost designer", but had I worn it to our last meeting in New York City? Hopefully she wouldn't remember.

There was only one thing I could be sure of. It was time to try out my home made blueberry pie.

The following evening we met as planned at Docks, where the best dressed set went in our small town. She spotted me and waved. Adoring fans were at her table, one of which was the owner. They disappeared as they saw me from her corner booth. She switched her back to the crowd swiftly and I witnessed her mood change from one of happy triumph to dismal anxiety and fear. It seemed one whole side of her face fell into the valley of despair. It only lasted a moment however, and there it was, the old Holly again. Her sense of recovery was still intact. It always had been her best feature.

"Are you all right?" was all I could say.

"I just need a vacation, that's all. How's that great family of yours, the new twins? You've always been the lucky one. You look fantastic!"

We laughed together as we remembered how we had been taught back at the academy to say "fantastic" instead of any of the more unusual four letter cuss words of that era. Father Fagan always insisted his girls were too upper class for any other designation.

Soon we were ordering from that unbeatable sea food menu and laughing over the arrogance of our youth. It would all be upward and onward for our select group, bad news for the rest of the world.

I had heard vague rumors of her recent marriage breakup and steered the conversation to optimism for her book tour. It didn't have the effect I had expected. She seemed to want to stay in the past.

We topped our great meal off with a desert that you could only dream of. Oh well, I thought, I'll play that game, if you like. We discussed fond memories, faceless cadets and overnight pajama parties. Yes, we thought we had invented them. Great times!

She came by cab, so I offered to drop her off, it was on my way.

"Will you and Robert come to my book signing tomorrow at the hotel?" It seemed more a command than a request, and a desperate one at that. I could only go if my son could pick me up. Surely she could understand that.

We exchanged good-byes, but not before the fright returned to her eyes. I released her lock and waved her out, fearing that long ride home in the dark.

Best to concentrate on my aversion to nighttime driving!

CHAPTER TWO

At the Taj

My son, Robert and I approached the Taj Mahal the following Saturday, as Holly requested. Winter in these shore cities is a bit of a hardship, but you wouldn't know it, seeing the crowds milling about the outside of the casino.

We parked the car in the underground garage and trudged our way to the lobby of the Taj. Then I saw it, a small announcement of the author HJ Hemmings, now meeting with fans for a recent autographed copy of her latest hit, "A Wrong Turn in My Sometimes Happy Life".

We followed directions and shortly found our way to this triumphal event. I had no trouble spotting my old friend Holly, she was, as usual surrounded by chatter and energy that seemed to have a mind of its own.

Busy travelers that seemed to be accustomed to plush surroundings were mindlessly milling around. They were, I supposed, used to the lives of celebrities as I had never been. Life, to me, sadly had always been one of hard work and figuring out how I'd reach the next level safely.

I was really happy and proud for Holly, she'd always had that energy I so badly lacked. It was my excuse in any case for my lack of success in any chosen field. If I'd really wanted to shoot for the stars, energy, that was what I lacked! Holly's explanation, she was always so tactful, "you were always just happy, just the two of you, and just the way you were." That was true, but now I had no excuses.

She spotted us and waved. This was the way I always thought of Holly, happily on top of it all, picking her way through the choices that abounded around her, not muddling through the way most of us were.

This beautiful face hadn't changed at all. Those eyes, mine never seemed to match, were elegant and animated. She'd applied just the right touch of color, no more, no less.

How did you get that perfect hair style to stay just the way it was last night? She couldn't have slept, it seemed as if it were an accent piece to set off the exquisite green silk suit, professional, yet not "off the rack". The face she wore was her success look which said, "I have arrived and am comfortably aware of it."

I looked down at my shoes with the low heels that I'd ordered over the internet with just a little help from my son, and wished I'd worn a different pair. Who cared if they were comfortable? Surely Holly's weren't! It must have taken some practice to swing one leg casually over the other just to keep them on.

My son Robert took off in search of a book that interested him while I waited patiently for my turn in line. My book was already signed and waiting for me at Holly's table.

"Robert looks great, you haven't been lying at all" came across the line. Then, when I got there, she whispered, "I'm almost through here, let's break out of here, walk the boards like we used to, eat some pizza, and check out the natives."

"Oh dear, those days are behind me and have been for quite some time" I thought to myself. "I don't think I'm quite what she's looking for at this time." The visit was a mistake, walking the boardwalk in this nippy weather. Did she realize how unlikely it was we'd find a quiet place to walk to for grey goose martinis in stiletto heels?

What a surprise! It was wonderful. Once we were out on the boardwalk, the salt air filled our nostrils as we drew our thick coats around us. We headed toward adventure, just as we used to, and found just the spot Holly was looking for, something about a pony. The crowd inside was beckoning us to join them in their celebration.

Just then I spotted the harsh looks from Robert. He seemed to be saying to me "You owe me one!" I'd seen that look more than once.

Out loud he said, "We really have to get back, you know tomorrow is my dinner at the church. It's Meet the Pastor night, and this place could get me disqualified". His eye glanced around the room at the other booths around us where the crowd was getting more than just a little loud.

We gave in to him, she a little more reluctantly than I. We escorted her back to the classy palms and through the lobby with the high columns of the Taj.

Outside of her room, Robert felt a little sorry for breaking up our evening so early. He tried to make up for it by inviting her to our dinner at the New Jerusalem church. Robert offered incentive with "the Rileys will pick you up in the lobby at six. You won't have to drive at all."

That clinched it for her. He was one of the most sensitive and thoughtful members of the human race. I knew he was just being polite.

She grabbed at the invitation, got the time and place, and promised to be there in the lobby.

I was more than just a little surprised, and didn't expect to see her there at all.

I should gave known better, something was wrong for sure. We were being pressured by Holly, who was really the expert at throwing a curve just at the right time, driving home the right pitch to the right ball.

The next evening, Holly walked into our dinner along with the Rileys, waving and carrying books for distribution. That big smile accompanied the grand entrance and the performance was about to begin.

Something had told me to be prepared. I had placed a setting beside my own. Our friendship was an old one. Once Holly had an idea, there was no stopping her. I just smiled. She had always made me laugh, and I needed that right now.

There is nothing better than an old fashioned, impromptu church dinner. The meal was fantastic, turkey or ham and a choice of six homemade pies. The impromptu part was an unexpected guest, a celebrity at that, just the thing to set off a great menu.

A quick Bible study quiz determined the lucky recipient of the newly signed novel, and Robert should have been proud of how well his young students did.

The congregation was thrilled. They had not expected to meet the New York Times best selling author of the year, nor had I.

After dinner we had quite a delightful recount of how easy it was, if you applied yourself to your writing, never gave up and did your chores regularly, you too could 'be an instant success. She had made me all charged up and ready to chart a book, and set up a regular routine for it. This would happen, of course, only after I planned an area where I could be comfortable writing.

A Wrong Turn of the Search for a Signing

Somehow I knew it would never happen, but I was really mega motivated. I was really surprised at how many of our church members had read her books.

They were really quite racy, but I enjoyed them.

Sorry about that folks of the church!

I was a loyal fan of Holly's, and always had been.

It was nice to know that some things never changed. How could I expect to know that changes were working their way behind the scenes, waiting for the least expected chance to appear!

CHAPTER THREE

At another overnight party

We stayed longer than we expected. It was one of our most successful dinners of the year. Holly was spectacular. Her local fans were all interested in her life, and were enjoying the particulars of her happy life on the circuit.

Ruth, Robert's wife and I walked Holly to the Riley's car, and I couldn't help but notice when we opened the door, her overnight bag was stored already in the back seat.

"I just thought I'd get a room around here. I've already sent my bags on ahead. I'm not familiar with the city, and I'm leaving in the morning. At the desk, they said I'd be closer to the airport around here."

Ruth quickly replied, "You're staying with us. We have plenty of room. Of course, you'll stay, don't even argue!" She didn't, as I expected.

Once at the manse, we bundled the twins into one of the twin beds, and, with me in the other, the children and I had an evening of telling ghost stories. Holly had the rare treat of having the guest room all to herself. We met later in the evening in the living room, both of us saw it as our last evening to catch up on what was new.

Holly stopped in the middle of what she was about to say "I can't tell you what it's like to be at peace at last. I think it

A Wrong Turn of the Search for a Signing

was the fun, the friends, and the prayers. Yes it's been a while since I've prayed last. I feel like a new person. I now feel like my good old self again. If that was ever any good, only God knows."

"Look, Angie, would you continue on to my next book signing? It's in Myrtle Beach, a great place, right on the ocean. It's the last one I have to visit, I'll be finished, go home, and you'll have a great view of the ocean. Please say yes."

The next morning, we settled it, my son, his wife and I in the war room to the left of the kitchen. "Mom, when was your last vacation? It could be fun."

I thought of the things I had planned, repairs in the laundry room and a visit to the chiropractor. Neither one of those things seemed like fun at all. What could it hurt?

The kids would look in on things for me, my chiropractor and the laundry room could wait. Why not help Holly celebrate her success?

It was final, I would fly down at the end of the week and that would give me time to worry about whether or not it was too hasty a plan.

We might not have another chance like this to enjoy a pretty beach view at the slow time of year and renew our friendship. It was, after all, my favorite time of the year to enjoy the ocean, it's once mighty and untamed power seemed to be plotting next years revenge.

Holly suggested I pack light and shop there, it might be fun she said.

I was truly not expecting the enthusiastic response to my need for a more interesting wardrobe. Was mine really that bad? Who knew?

The following morning Robert and I drive Holly to the AC Airport. We saw her safely make connections to her flight. At the same time we made reservations for a trip to Charleston where I could visit in-laws I hadn't seen in some time and follow with a bus trip to Myrtle Beach.

Luckily they had vacancies at the Hampton Inn there. I had been there before. An imitation boardwalk had been designed to make you think you were at the beach, though you were far from it. Always lots of fun, if you liked the boardwalk experience, which I did.

It wasn't until the ride back that Robert confided that he felt Holly was holding back something that was scaring her. He had always been intuitive about others. It was what made him so well loved by his congregation. At least I felt that way.

"Mom, I think she needs to talk to someone, and soon. She was about to share something with me when she had second thoughts and retreated. There's something there that's new. Just do me a favor, be there for her." Over the years he'd had brief encounters with her, but it was a part of the past he'd always enjoyed.

I had a fleeting moment of fear. It gripped my being and traveled down to the toes of my feet with lightning speed.

His statement matched my very thoughts. How could both of us pick up on the same thing, something was terribly wrong!

The flight on Thursday was uneventful. I have never liked flying. It seems unnatural. After getting help stowing my small baggage overhead, I grabbed my new, privately signed copy of one of the biggest hits on the Times recommended reading list, and to my total surprise, I lost myself in it. It was one of the best and hottest novels I'd read in a long time.

It had everything, from frankly hot sex to an unexpectedly high-jacked husband. How in the world could anyone predict this in the orderly life I seemed to have led?

A Wrong Turn of the Search for a Signing

A noisy child appeared to be much distressed and I was forced to put aside my novel.

I'd finish it later, which to my regret I never did do.

CHAPTER FOUR

Off we go into the wild blue yonder

The plane was noiselessly headed south, slicing its way through the clouds of beautiful Virginia. I had stashed my antique carry on and settled back to enjoy the quite ride to South Carolina. Meanwhile my thoughts were contemplating the happy memories that Holly and I had enjoyed together in our carefree college days.

We were impetuous, not roommates exactly but we shared a common shower room and soon discovered how much we were mistaken for one another, yes we looked alike in our towel covered heads after a shower. It lead to a friendship where, just to confuse others, we styled and colored our hairstyles to match. We had even double dated and switched partners to see how far we could get away with it. What fools! I did have too much time on my hands after all.

The overhead lights and message from the pilot that we were entering tremulous weather broke my reverie and I picked up my copy of "A Wrong Turn" so I could answer any questions put to me. I found myself completely immersed in reviewing the novel instead. No wonder she had such a following. The heroine found herself in the middle of escapes

A Wrong Turn of the Search for a Signing

from one battle to anther, between identity theft and terror. This was a new direction for Holly. Was no one to be safe in this uncertain landscape?

Before I knew it, my thoughts were rudely interrupted and I had to prepare to depart. The kind stewardess helped me with my overnight and without further incident I arrived at Charleston Airport.

I needn't have worried about finding out how to transfer to the train station as I had a welcoming committee of my in-laws and, oh yes, the loud cries of "Hi Angie, over here!" from my old friend Holly. Why was she here? Oh well, it must been a lull in her busy life. In any case I was glad for the support. I was unused to traveling and welcomed the company.

The four of us had no trouble finding a small seafood café nearby, and sure enough, that at least hadn't changed. Our shrimp and prawns were spectacular. We had no trouble catching up on what was going on in our lives. My younger brother and his wife were still enjoying Charleston life. Not much had changed there. He was still working at the airport.

Holly just listened and announced we wouldn't be taking a train at all. A limo would be meeting us and driving us up to our destination. Oh the ever loving lifestyles of the rich and famous. How would I get used to living down home without them.

If the past was any clue at all, I would adjust. I always had.

I slid into the back seat of the limo and sunk into the cushy back seat. This trip was starting to look up as I breathed my first sigh of relief in a month.

Quick goodbyes followed and the sleek Cadillac travelled powerfully and quietly into the night, while Holly and I slept in the back seat.

My small bag stood alone with a stylish garment bag which I'd never seen in the classy lobby. The lobby was exactly as I remembered, the feel of the beachfront with none of the inconveniences. I climbed into my comfortable bed and slept like a baby after I checked in at the ground floor lobby.

The following morning, I read the note left on my table that Holly would have me picked up the next day, which was today, by Richard, Holly's driver. "Where had he been in Atlantic City"?

I took a peek into the garment bag and got the surprise of my life, a wonderful selection of designer suits, from silk to wool, daytime to nighttime. I tried on my favorite and enjoyed the new me in the mirror, eventually wearing one of them down to the dining room for breakfast. Yes, I'd made it to the fast lane. I picked up my biscuit and stared through the glass doors at the fake palm trees.

Meanwhile, some months back, in one of those lovely, crooked backstreets in San Francisco clear across the country, a very somber scenario was being played out on the fourth floor of the Wharton building.

Three graying gentlemen in Seville Row suits were in deep conversation around a steel and glass top table. No one looked particularly happy. A very unpleasant decision would have to be made, no more putting it off.

"She's got to be cut, her work isn't what it used to be. The readers won't stand for it and neither will the bank."

"I say give it one more shot. Her new manager says she's been cruising, but she's rested and ready to go again. This new one is the brass ring, he says. Best seller."

Outside the room was heard the sound of a printer revving up. Who knew what would be born today. Three serious heads were anxious to find out. One could only hope!

A Wrong Turn of the Search for a Signing

The fate of the great HC Hemmings was being determined by this influential trio. When the printer was finished spitting out this new novel, a sigh of relief would pass around the room. Holly was well liked and now she was back!

CHAPTER FIVE

At the signing

The lobby of the Hilton was festive that day. Signs pointed to a popular fiction writer having a best selling book signing that day. The hum and buzz sent the crowds to a handsome door off the main path.

An irate gentleman was headed to the focal point of the crowd. "The famous HJ Hemmings is in town, all right," he thought. I'll do something about that!.

He stood back a while, noticing the lines approaching the two figures that were seated behind an exquisite console table They seemed to be enjoying the celebrity status of the afternoon. Standing behind one of its ornate columns nearby, he listened in for a while, before deciding how to handle the unfortunate encounter which would inevitably occur.

"You two must be sisters" came from one of the well heeled women in the enthusiastic line which formed in his view.

"She's my older sister, Angie, and she just came in from Charleston."

"Older? Those treatments in Europe must really be working," came from the unfortunate occupant of the chair located next to her, who was about to leave in protest.

"I'm joking, Angie. Why can't you see that?"

A Wrong Turn of the Search for a Signing

It was a good time for the foreigner from another state to interfere. "Can I ask what you are doing here?" he asked angrily as he confronted Holly.

Holly had difficulties on both sides, she was outnumbered. She placed the "Be Back Soon" sign on the table, grabbed her publisher by the sleeve and left the scene as she saw the confused hosts start to appear.

Once they were comfortably hidden from the crowd, Holly got her answer.

"The office called and said they needed more books here. You can imagine how surprised I was, knowing you agreed to cancel. I was supposed to be your replacement. Your doctor suggested it, and I believed him like a fool. I let you handle the details. I also know you did the show in Atlantic City. What's going on?"

"I'm feeling much better now. Can't you see what a success the book is? Don't argue with success. Did you bring more books? Good!"

Before he had a chance to tell her that this was the reason that corporate had decided to end its relationship, she'd run back to her perch. She was becoming too irrational, too difficult to control, and frankly her work was not quite what it used to be. That this novel had come along when it did was fortunate. It saved her neck. It was, in fact, the best work she'd done in years. Could it happen again? No one was sure.

"I'm sorry Angie", as she turned to her friend, "My doctors were wrong. I've been feeling great and too much work went into my plans. I guess we got our messages crossed. It happens."

The lighthearted banter continued throughout the afternoon. She had soothed her friend's outraged feathers, she was an avowed expert at that. While she signed her last few books, they made plans to go to a show at the Hilton to make this whole trip worth the effort.

`"Oh come on, let's have fun. First let me go and make peace with the office. These office people are always so up tight."

And that is exactly what they set out to do. Angie looked down at the greatest outfit she would wear again in years and set her sights on doing just that!

Just at that moment, a voice cried out from the line, "You're definitely much younger! Is Antoine ever going to fall in love?", which made Angie cry out "Only if Holly wants him to, and she might." She was beginning to get into the act with Holly. She had to laugh. No wonder Holly wanted to be here with these crazy fans.

The next morning in her room at the Hampton Inn, Angie looked across at the Tico Taco and the beautiful boardwalk. She was surprised again that there was no ocean view, but could see the crowds had arrived early. No, wait, they were still there from the night before. They were not crowds, but people in happy gear ready to go on partying.

She made coffee in the complicated machine the room provided, and sat at the window to review the strange events of the day before. Her old friend had changed very much.

No surprise there. She seemed a little meaner, but a little more unsure of herself, in short, it was still a question over the wisdom of this trip.

Although promises were made by Holly to tell her the whole story, no attempt at all had been made to do so! She'd had plenty of opportunity to do just that, though dinner turned out to be a nightclub act, very entertaining. It was far from a quiet background to provide for a long talk. No explanation was forthcoming, except to say that her husband of so many years had left her.

A Wrong Turn of the Search for a Signing

This was the explanation she had been waiting for, the great exposure Holly had promised that would set the record straight. She said she had become tired of the tight schedules and the demanding hours she'd had to agree to. It had all made her feel tired and eventually unglued, no wonder Guy had left. "You know! It was both that and his usual girl thing."

She was not ready to talk about it, the wounds were too raw. Please give her time to work it out in her own mind, she'd pleaded.

She could do that, if that was all that was needed. One more day and Angie was out of there. She looked at the happy hangovers on the crowds on that fake boardwalk. Yes, It was all fake after all. That and she was so homesick for Ocean City and the dear people who made sense, the same sense, year after year.

Suddenly, it wasn't wonderful at all.

On the other hand, how great would it be to cause a publisher to fly across the country just to talk business? The next day she expected more of the same and made hasty preparations to pack. Perhaps she could move up the tickets a day and get out of there. Holly was no longer the person she had known in college. What did she expect?

Angellica was nothing if not someone who stuck to her promises, so she dressed for her last act in this unhappy story. She grabbed the second of the beautiful outfits her friend had provided and once again she felt herself to be the recipient of newfound wealth.

She found, as she arrived in this luxurious hotel, a magnificent room she was totally unprepared for. She sat next to Holly, who had to call on her cell-phone to make arrangements for the day with Richard. In her imperious way of offending without meaning to do so, Hollly had pinnacled to perfection with age.

Unfortunately, this lapse of professional image had taken its toll.

She forgot, in her confusion, to turn off her cell-phone. An incoming call abruptly interrupted this stream of commands as Holly attempted to hang up.

She grabbed the call. Angie was not even aware that she possessed a cell-phone.

It had been turned off all this time.

"Guy, I can't talk now. It's not a good time. I'll call later!" She cut him off as abruptly as she had answered.

Was this the response of a woman who was grieving over the loss of a loved one? Perhaps she was justifiably rattled, or even better, she was truly hiding her emotions with great theatrical talent.

Angie had the impression that a lot more than that would have been said if she hadn't been in the room. Marriages, who could explain them?

Especially marriages that had been cast in concrete for thirty or more years! This one was about to tumble if she knew anything at all.

Soon she'd be home and this would be a forgotten chapter in an otherwise happy play.

CHAPTER SIX

Deep in the night

In the early foggy morning, which customarily happened in those wintry Lake George blizzard seasons, bitter frozen breathing came out in spurts. The lonely figure cut a trail through the frozen brush.

Only the slight sliver of moon cast its light on the shadowy scene taking place on the secluded edge of the lake. Gone were the happy crowds of summer visitors and the laughter of children which made their way from the hot, stuffy cities.

This lonely figure was not alone, but dragging a burlap bag atop a sled across the light patches of snow mingled with leaves through the leafless wooded area.

It reached a small boat moored loosely along the shore, dragged the coarse bag from the sled, hoisted it into the boat, and dropped to the ground panting.

The darkly clad figure stared into space recounting the steps of the previous weeks which had lead up to this stark moment.

This was the easy part. The hard part was over, waiting for the perfect time to remove the body, after the last of the daily employees left for the winter season. Those better known were the first to go, after the pattern of prior years. Someone always seemed to be hanging around.

Safe at last, sliding the body down the front carpeted stairway was physically no challenge. Staying in shape had been a lifetime problem of visiting gyms, no problem there.

Out to the wide porch along the lake view, and through the broken lattice which covered the strong planks holding up the Victorian porch! The bundle was dropped to the ground and shoved under the porch without much thought or sentiment.

"Now get on to making plans for winterizing the remote buildings". This had been done routinely over the past twenty years. Once again, no problem, the vacation homestead would be secure as ever.

Much better to move the heavy parcel to the old shed, which hadn't been used in years.

First of all, buy a stronger lock.

After a prolonged last look at the lake on the old wicker loveseat, the figure moved inside for a last chance at the warm living room before the pipes were wire wrapped and the phone disconnected.

The suitcases were already packed in the Rover along with the technical accessories for the laptop.

This was all being planned and an exit route was in the making. Now get into the Rover and head toward the Interstate for a warm meal and a safe motel room.

There was a smug satisfaction for a job well done, so far at least!

This would do for a while until plans could be made to secure a better final location, the old boat house was the best bet. It was full of holes and hiding places.

As if in agreement, a hand slid outside of the bundle, and dragged helplessly along the ground to its final resting place as the silent figure rushed into the anonymous woods.

CHAPTER SEVEN

On the road again

The giant Trailblazer bus was headed noiselessly along interstate 95 headed south with its small assortment of holiday travelers. One of them, Mrs. Peterson was slowly awakening from a drowsy nap, and for the moment was unsure of where she was.

Yes, the present was beginning to assert itself. A background of noisy hotel lobbies and smart conversation, totally alien to her usual way of life, was slowly coming to the surface. She was recalling the past few days in a haze of clouds surrounding a hub of hasty movement through space travel. Was she really here?

She knew now why she was on a Trailblazer, it seemed a reasonable thing to do, taking advantage of her brief time in the south to make a holiday visit to her younger brother. That last visit had been too brief. A small time out to Hilton Head Island, where he had a vacation home could be made and with very little effort.

"You know, I really shouldn't be traveling alone at my age" she was telling herself.

"I do wish there was coffee" as she continued the narration. She was routing around in her bag and came up with some chocolate and trail mix. "That would be Holly for sure" and while at it, another one of her many generous gifts, a small grey cell-phone.

"I can't believe you travel without one!" Holly had expressed when they were inside the small phone store in Myrtle Beach.

"Well, I don't, because I don't travel" she asserted.

They went to the small store because Holly had gone to get adjustments made on her cell-phone. While there, she made the grand gesture.

Angellica became a member of her "friends and family" circle. They could be in constant contact with each other whether Angie liked it or not. It had always been easier to go along with Holly's plans than to resist. She could always change it later on to a plan of her own making. She used to do just that. They added six or seven phone numbers to Angie's new phone that she would need on her bus trip and headed outside.

Back on the bus, Angie munched on her trail mix and her eyes were drawn to a couple in the front of the bus. They were sleepily leaning on one another with a small child between them.

"That used to be us, Rob and I traveling toward our future together with small Robert between us. It didn't really matter where we were going, we went there together".

Angie tried her new toy. No signal. Yes, even she had heard about that. Oh well, I do hope that rest room in the back of the bus works better than my new phone!

A muffled dog barking signal met her return to her seat which truly baffled Angie to the utmost. She could not imagine the origins of this sound. A string of obscenities belted out from the innocent looking phone once she figured out how to answer it. Some of the words she heard were beyond the scope of her understanding. She'd never heard them expressed quite in this way.

A Wrong Turn of the Search for a Signing

"Call your lawyer, Babe", emerged amid the thunderous bolt of the response.

"I'm not going to listen to this any more!" Angie closed her phone onto the seat with a furious slam, not caring whether she'd broken it or not.

When her mood became calmer, she brought the phone out again and studied the entries. This was not her phone.

The voice was Guy and he was not in possession of his good boy manners. It appeared she, Angie, was in possession of Holly's phone and the history of her last few conversations in South Carolina. She was in the midst of a major clash of property rights with Guy, Holly's husband of years. No wonder she didn't want any further dialog with him.

Angie ran to the front of the bus. No matter where she was headed, she wanted no more of this journey!

Home sounded better than ever. She needed to hear Robert's voice, and she needed that right now!

CHAPTER EIGHT

At the bus terminal

I was back in the unhappy present standing firmly in the Visitors Center of the Savannah bus terminal. The likewise unhappy driver had answered my wishes. I found myself explaining my difficult situation to the young clerk in an Elves stocking cap. It was about as festive as a bus terminal can become in a season's instant. I realized that I barely represented the seasoned traveler with my handcrocheted cap and jogging pants. Nevertheless there was that expensive dress carrier that raised an interesting thought. Who was this person?

What was he saying, this person dressed like an elf?

"Treetops, they have a vacancy. You'll love it there! Close to the tourist sights, yet out of the way of traffic".

"I'll take it, it'll be fine." Now I could call Robert and make him believe I was just where I'd planned to be all along.

A cab was called, and my bags followed along with me. I was about to find out where Savannah was and what it was like. I'd spend an evening at a place called Treetops and pretend to be in control of my life. Otherwise I would force my son to fly down to a place called Savannah and cause unnecessary expense.

Best of all I could tell Robert I now knew all the ins and outs of travel. That is, once I was safely situated.

A Wrong Turn of the Search for a Signing

Unfortunately he already knew Holly and I had messed up on the cell-phone purchase. How much he knew was anyone's guess, but he always seemed to find out, one way or another.

His first question was, as I knew it would be, "where are you? Everyone is looking for you."

It would be nice to be assured when I reached my destination at Treetop that everyone was looking for me.

Holly had called Robert and told him I was going to Hilton Head Island. She felt terrible about the phone switch, and said it was all her fault, but told him she would use her GPS to locate me.

What is she talking about? I'm going to call the folks in the morning and tell them not to worry. Now Angie, get to your new hotel and get some sleep!

At that we pulled up to the most beautiful pre-civil war townhouse I had ever seen. It wasn't a hotel at all, but a part of the past, a past I couldn't even conceive of.

Who were these lucky people who could own both one of these townhouses and a plantation outside of town at the same time? My driver, whose name was Sam, promised to tell me all about it. He gave me his card and I carefully packed it away in my purse.

Back to the idea of sleep! It sounded like the best plan I'd heard all day. I felt like one of those lucky people I had just questioned, one of those lucky ones of the forgotten era.

The room was clean and beautiful. The sheets were lilac scented and I planned to sleep like a baby surrounded by apple blossoms under a lace canopy.

As I fell into a deep sleep, I carried my fantasy one step further.

I had visions of my new life with admiring fans all around, each struggling to be the closest friend of the New York Times person of the year!

With all of these new outfits, it seemed I'd been waiting years for this prophetic event. Perhaps I'd add character to my nose and widen the eyes. It was called an eyelift, I think.

Best yet, I should look into renewing my passport.

There was one problem. I didn't have one. Better fix that situation first.

CHAPTER NINE

Along the Inter Coastal

There were signs of a winter chill all along the Inter Coastal waterway. The trees along the shore were newly stripped of their foliage and the sure hands of the captain of his small racing yacht pulled into a boatyard he'd known for many years. He'd had it in mind all along the difficult trip down from the tiny town in Lake George, he knew the ins and outs as no one else could.

He steered the small cabin cruiser into a small slip and headed inside the tiny office where he knew he'd have no trouble negotiating an all cash deal with the promise of a purchase a few months down of a craft that was just what he had in mind. So glad they had just what he needed. He'd return and seal the deal shortly.

The owner dropped him in front of a car rental to make his plans complete. A Buick would be just fine.

Next, Guy looked around the third rate economy class motel he found himself in.

It was clean, but certainly beneath the luxury he had become used to, The towels had been hanging too long, and they certainly were not as fresh as he'd like them to be. Only the location was perfect. Time to move on to the next step.

That was far from his greatest problem at the moment, The market was in freefall, and he had chosen an unlikely brokerage to hold his priceless portfolio, Leheman Brothers. They were not even answering the phones. Not a good sign. Luckily he had a smaller account not known to his friends and family in Canada, but it was entirely in his own name.

The sale of his California home in Bakersfield hadn't gone well. They insisted on calling his wife and hearing from her that the sale should go through. There was a problem with secondary mortgages and apparently he had one. She agreed as long as they put a generous check in her personal account, so she could buy a Cadillac she had in mind. It didn't put much in his account after the suspicious broker took her generous share.

He went outside into the still night and unloaded his new rental, which included a handsome piece of luggage, a small case from the glove compartment which held his piece, and an obscure brown bag with sustenance to help him through the night.

He was tired. He'd come down earlier in the day in his yacht, a 50 foot Maveric which he'd driven himself along the Intercoastel Waterway. He'd spend two days in the Maveric, starting on the Delaware Bay. From there it was easy to visit his wife, and when he'd left her she was resting comfortably in the clinic outside of Princeton, in Menlo Park.

The next day they called from the clinic and told him they had no idea where she was, she'd signed herself out and left with a person she called Richard. He was her driver, she claimed at the desk, and said they were leaving for lunch in town. They didn't return. He'd already missed the signing she'd had in Atlantic City and the one they'd both planned in Myrtle Beach.

A Wrong Turn of the Search for a Signing

It had taken some time to track the two of them down. One of them had ordered three cases of books, and they'd delivered two of them. He' didn't know where the third was going, but it would be close by he was sure.

It was Richard again, he'd caused all the trouble. He'd probably told Holly that her book had already been published, and it would be a success. He had the knowledge of how to order her books and how to set up a book signing. He's done it for her in the past. Who knew how much he knew?

It was time to put an end to Richard. The handsome face turned ugly and hard as the new plan was forming with an ever growing insanity.

Tomorrow was soon enough to call the publisher and arrange a place to pick up his check.

All of this wouldn't have been needed if his wife hadn't left the clinic. Wives, could they ever be counted on to do the right thing?

CHAPTER TEN

Angellica at the breakfast club

The sun came through the blinds in my sunny room to remind me that I had a great deal of work to do this morning, and not much time to do it. Yesterday was totally wasted, I had been consumed by unfortunate events drawn by my fears of strange places leading to even stranger places. In short, that was why I didn't travel much.

Luckily I was the only one in the Treetop Bed and Breakfast and I didn't have to face unknown guests over gingerbread and eggs, or whatever they served. I slyly took off with a muffin and coffee, though in a different mood I would have enjoyed the Victorian sideboard with its assortment of goodies.

Right now I needed the privacy of my cheerful room with the apple blossom wallpaper. I'd better think hard and decide what to do with that horrible cellphone that had brought me to this scary time and place. First I had to find my old friend, something was terribly wrong. All of my senses told me this was the case.

The facts were these: Holly was avoiding it, but whatever "it" was, she was incapable of concentrating on a singe thought process. She constantly changed the subject back to her novels and the characters in them. It was as if they were the only

A Wrong Turn of the Search for a Signing

reality she chose to deal with, but they were still only faceless characters in a fantasy in her past.

Before doing anything else, I wanted to get in touch with someone in the land of the living. I picked up the cell-phone and hit one of the entries in Holly's messages. It seemed to be a law office. Holly's last instruction by her husband had been to call her lawyer. The phone rang right on cue.

It was answered professionally and the call was transferred immediately. A deep voice answered with an abrupt "Where are you?" Not wanting to steer anyone wrong, I immediately protested with "This is not Holly. I have her phone by mistake. I'd like you to pass on a message to her that I have her phone and will hold it for her."

The message was noted, with the addition that she talk her friend into calling him or his office as least. It was urgent that he speak with her, her husband wished to make some adjustments to the property settlement. They didn't seem at all unreasonable, but they should be addressed.

I assured him I would do so just as soon as possible then I promptly hung up.

The next call was to an entry that seemed to be a doctor's office. Once again the same result appeared. After finding out where I was calling from, I admitted I was not Holly but wanted the same message passed on to her.

After I received a similar response, with the additional response that my friend was in need of medical care, they stressed the need that Holly respond back promptly should I speak to my friend.

So much for telling the truth, that's not the way to get information, I thought.

Surprise! Her friend was on the line with the next incoming call. "I'm so sorry for the mess up. I bought a new phone and very few of my friends have the number. Ignore anyone who calls. I'm fine, never felt better! There's an Omni in the area, and it's where I'm going next. I'll call you once I've made final arrangements. Enjoy Savannah, it's beautiful and the people are *great*".

*That is e*xactly what I decided to do. I dressed, called Sam after I found his card and went to its shopping area.

Sam gave me a short tour of the mile square town, which was breathtakingly beautiful. It must be gorgeous in spring when the blossoms were out.

I treated myself nest to a henna rinse with a very futuristic cut and purchased a small mud pack to finish off my evening alone in my new hideaway. I stopped at a small café and had some good southern cooking, served by a friendly waitress. That hadn't happened in a long time.

It felt so good to have my hair done. I stopped to think about my situation while in the café next door. I had some really good reasons for being thankful.

Neither Holly's lawyer nor her doctor sounded desperate. They were mildly interested, but not intensely so. Holly was safe, at least she sounded safe.

Angie gathered her packages together and hailed a cab for the Treetops B & B.

As she entered the pretty establishment, she was met by the owner with "Your son will be here tomorrow", followed by, "you look terrific!"

My son would want me to cut short my stay in Savannah, and I was fond of these friendly people.

As I looked around the room, I had the most pleasant experience. All the walnut moldings were covered in sprays of fir and pine cones. They were decorating early and the sight

A Wrong Turn of the Search for a Signing

was spectacular. After a moment of sheer genius, she asked, "Do you have a pick up laundry service?"

"Oh yes, but it takes up to three days" was the answer she expected.

"I'll go and get my things," I responded.

That would buy some time in this unbelievably spirited place. I had solved my problem.

I looked at the space that had been cleared in the old fashioned parlor. It had obviously been cleared as the future sight of a Christmas tree. In my mind's eye I had a childish desire to be part of this Christmas party being prepared, and I could see stockings all hung by the chimney with care.

I went upstairs, dressed, and slept like a child. "Yes, Virginia, there is a Santa Clauses!

What would tomorrow bring?

CHAPTER ELEVEN

The trail picks up steam

Guy checked out of the room and moved all of his belonging back into rental Buick, the suitcase, the carrier with his best suit in it, and most important of all, the small pistol which he placed again into the glove compartment.

Only the brown bag was gone. It had served its purpose in this classless room. After a haircut which he badly needed, he'd find this Bed and Breakfast in Savannah, called Treetop and get directions to Holly's next signing, wherever that was.

It was important that he appear casual and successfully dressed as he met with someone called Angellica, the one she or Richard had changed phones with.

Anxious about his wife, yes, he'd tell her about the doctor's verdict and that the clinic and the state police had an all point's call for her safe return. Unfortunately, that part was not true. He'd told them not to worry, he was meeting his wife as they'd agreed, and would return together with her over the weekend.

He turned the ignition key of the smooth Buick. It made no noise as it started toward Savannah. He was glad he'd left the final arrangements for the yacht up in the air. It might be better if he returned with his wife and headed up the Inter Coastal with her. It always had a good effect of their marriage

A Wrong Turn of the Search for a Signing

when he was at the helm and she had nothing on her mind but the fresh wind in her hair.

Yes, he was back in control again, and all was well with the world.

He stared straight ahead at the taillights as the interstate faded away into the future. It was like his future, unsure but feeling better with the passage of each mile along the heavily treed interstate.

The only thing he was sure of, Richard would have to be removed from the picture. He didn't think it would cause too much of a stir, he had had brushes with the law in the past.

It was the only explanation of his loyalty to Holly and his inability to find other employment.

He had no idea that his plans were about to be turned upside down by events he had no control over. He had never met the lady from Sea Isle City.

CHAPTER TWELVE

A new dimension for Angellica

The next morning in the inn, I looked out of my picturesque window down upon Forsythe Park, which piece of information I had recently become aware of. In the two days I'd been in Savannah, I knew little more than that it was steeped in history and romantic in its beauty. In the background arose a tall church spiral to let me know who was really in charge here. The church seemed to hold all the mysteries of the south. But it brought me no closer to mine.

Could this be the famous Garden of Good and Evil so popular years ago? If so, how appropriate! Where did I put Sam's card? I needed another tour.

I had a full plate ahead of me and it all centered around the only clue I had, Holly's cell phone.

I wished I knew more about these devilish instruments of torture. I'd tried it once, but tired of the repeated sales calls while driving. Neither Holly's doctor nor lawyer knew that she was missing, or was she? Another thing to consider, was Holly behind the switch of the cells? She was one of the smartest of their crowd, back in the day, and it certainly eliminated unpleasant calls from her husband.

After a large southern fried breakfast, I invaded the small office of the Treetop. I decided to ask innocently for help with the new gadget which I'd come into unexpectedly. The pretty young clerk sympathetically showed me the clicks I had to make to return the calls. She told me her name was Tina should I need her again. Tina explained why I hadn't been able to hear anything but a "dead zone" which, depending on the service I had, only responded to towers in the area. Very clever, I thought. I wanted to be alone should Holly try to call, so I hurried out of the room.

To my great surprise, Holly did so right away, the crazy dog barked on cue. "I'm worried about you", I said. "Your doctor and lawyer both want to see you right away"

"Oh forget it. I feel much better since I've quit taking those pills. They made me feel dizzy and confused. As for my lawyer, he's representing that scoundrel, and as soon as I have time, I'm getting my own, lawyer and that's it! I'll call again!" She hastily hung up.

Next, I found a comfortable chair in the festive room. Christmas decorating was in full force and I was hoping the music and decorations would invade the funk I felt throughout my small frame.

Something could not remove the cold sinister chill I was beginning to get in the small of my back, evil was not far behind. I had a fully developed sense of disaster that never failed me. I knew that only too well. My sense of foreboding was making itself felt and demanding to be heard. It would not be silenced.

First things first, call my son and tell him to wait a few days, surely the laundry was slow in these small towns. I'd found a comfortable and cheerful place to stay, and I intended to do just that.

Just then that nasty dog barked again, and I hastily answered it. "Thank goodness!" the faceless voice answered. "I've been trying to reach you forever".

It was an alumni association associate, and they were planning their first reunion of Margaret's class. They wanted to reach her, and this was her last known number, one that could be reached at least. Those associations were so persistent, thought Angie. So odd that they couldn't reach Margaret on the island!

"I'll have her call you" and I hung up. I wasn't sure what to say to this request until I knew the facts a little better.

I brought out Holly's cell phone and studied the recent calls both from Margaret and to her. Funny that they all disappeared at about the same time, they seemed to end just after Holly left the lodge at the end of the season. If she had run away with Guy, wouldn't she take her cell with her? These persistent alumni chasers should have reached her somehow. Oh dear! So much for those tiny cells that were developing mightily into storm clouds right here on the horizon!

I dressed in my old mom jeans and went into town, the Historic District they called it. I felt like a good walk would do me some good, and I had more shopping to do. I would really like to be here under different conditions. If this nasty situation could be cleared up, I was really up for it. What miracle had brought me to this wonderful place?

This town had such an uplifting effect on me, especially with the decorations they were installing, all Christmas fir and cedar and snow flakes, fake ones but still snow flakes.

It was all about the excitement in the air as these town folks were preparing for the expected holiday cheer.

Some time later as I returned to the small cheerful inn, I was immediately met by an unexpected stranger. Had someone

A Wrong Turn of the Search for a Signing

looked down from the church spire nearby and ordered a priest for me?

At once I realized that the beautifully tailored black overcoat had drawn me to that conclusion.

To my great relief it was Guy. "Where is she, she may be in trouble!" I melted as he apologized for the cell-phone mix up.

To nobody's surprise he was still as handsome as ever, classic features with salt and pepper hair. It was all styled to match his thousand dollar shoes. He'd found me through tracking that blasted phone.

"Let's talk in here," as I let him to an unoccupied room downstairs at the inn.

For some reason my old trust returned. This was the only person who could answer my persistent question of where Holly was right now, and why.

"All I know is that she's with Richard", was my answer to his distressed plea.

"What's HE doing here"? He was obviously baffled.

"He seems to be her driver. I thought you would know that. Who exactly is he"?

Guy's handsome face became changed into something I'd never seen in him, something unfamiliar, fear combined with complete bewilderment.

"She doesn't have a driver. He's her former secretary and sometime manager, not that she could really be managed with this new illness! It's early Parkinson's. That's the latest diagnosis. It's still being analyzed."

He continued "Since her illness, she's really become defiant and irrational. She claimed Richard was not putting her thoughts down as she stated, but was deliberately messing up her narration. Holly fired him".

I told him that he, Guy, was being seen as the reason for the quick departure of Margaret from the island and the reason for his quick departure with her as well.

At this point, I was merely guessing. Holly had only hinted at it, but had never stated it as fact.

"His usual girl thing", as she had expressed it, but her whole expression had indicated that this was not an isolated incident! This had not been the first time he had not been faithfull, I knew Holly well enough to know that, at least.

I saw a quick change in Guy's appearance, and there was no faking it, he was alarmed. He assured me he had never found the girl interesting or attractive. What could anyone have been thinking who could have promoted that idea and who could have lied so to Holly?

It was making sense now. His active mind was soaring. Things were beginning to make a clear pattern in his mind, things that didn't make any sense at all. A new horror was emerging. Guy was putting his overcoat back on and heading for the door.

I was going with him. That was the only thing I was sure of right now.

"No one seems to know where Margaret is, she's disappeared. We thought she was with you."

I could understand his panic. I went into the office and explained my sudden change of plans with Tina. She would pass on my news.

Somehow Tina didn't seem surprised. She just shook her head and went on with her typing.

CHAPTER THIRTEEN

The story unfolds in the car

Guy continued this strange turn of events as he drove the long interstate while staring straight ahead, unblinking. He continued his narrative.

"Holly's response to her doctor's explanation of her mood changes and erratic behavior didn't surprise me. She dug in with strong denial. When she fired Richard, things had really become dangerous, and I found excuses to spend longer times in the city."

"Her good nature won out, and in the end, she let him take care of the old lodge while he found something better. Closing down at summers end was always a big job, and he was aware of all that it involved, wire wrapping the pipes and dismissing the employees. In short, he had a place to stay. That's all I know, the last place the three were known to be together was at the lodge. I wish now that my anger wasn't the last thing I'd expressed. I could have been more patient."

"She's in trouble Angie! What should I do?"

The smooth Buick turned into a situation room. As if on cue, the phone in my purse rang out with that crazy ring of a barking dog.

I knew in my bones that it was Holly. It had to be, thank you Lord!

"Please tell me where you are. You're in great danger," as I answered.

"I'm back at the hotel. I forgot my phone back in my room, at least I think I did. Richard and I were about to get more cash, but I won out, he turned around. Next I'm coming to see you."

Thank all that was holy, Richard knew better than to disobey her orders. Once he had that cash, things would be different, but not now.

"Do you trust me Holly? Follow my instructions. Can you bolt the door? Do it now!" There was a quiet hush.

I could only hope that's what she would do.

There was no sound at the other end. A voice returned to the phone.

"Did you do it? Did you bolt the door?" I said anxiously.

"Tell me what's wrong?"

"Pick up the phone in the room, hit operator and ask for security to come to your room quickly".

I waited while the sounds of movement could he heard. I heard banging on the door and they seemed to be calling out "Security". It was becoming increasingly louder.

"Margaret is missing, only Richard seems to know where she is" I told her.

I turned the phone over to Guy, I was simply out of ideas, and he was explaining the situation to the security team.

He was saying that the person about to approach the room might be responsible for a murder in Lake George and that his wife was ill. There was an attempted kidnapping.

He hung up when he seemed satisfied and turned his inquiry to a west coast publishing firm.

For the rest of that long drive to the hotel where security directed us, we put the time to good use, only talking of one

A Wrong Turn of the Search for a Signing

thing, what had gone so wrong in the successful history of HJ Hemmings, that once successful author and speaker.

The next call by Guy was to the accounting firm, Brown & Brothers. A check was sent out to them that morning and Holly would be there is pick it up at their North Charleston Office. We had really cut it close!

As we continued the drive, I had time for one more try to get Robert on the phone. I couldn't do it. We were out of range.

"Do you think Holly could have recognized a novel she had never written?"

His answer didn't surprise me at all, "No, not at all!"

I had never seen my friend's problem as clinical but had been preoccupied with my own foolish whims and fantasies. Please forgive me Holly, was all I could think.

Suddenly I could see who had switched phones and why. Richard had been running the whole show all along, except for that brief episode in New Jersey.

Holly had thrown in a trip to see her old friend at the last minute. It had undone Richard's plans, thank Heaven!

Richard was a great actor. He had fooled me completely with those stark thick eyebrows and cold dark eyes that showed no emotion.

That quiet reserve of his combined with total reticence had completely masked a plot to kidnap my friend!

I was now en route to thwart his evil plan. Hopefully we would arrive on time!

CHAPTER FOURTEEN

A strange turn of events

The sleek Buick was traveling noiselessly along Interstate 95 toward our ultimate destination of Charleston. The quiet purr of the engines, the soft leather seats and the magnificent high powered dashboard, all lead to a soft dozing in my mind. We were about to bring our story to a swift conclusion. My friend was safe and my world was at peace.

Guy's handsome face stared straight ahead to our final destination. This was a man who was used to being in command of the situation. I could see how Holly had let herself be controlled for so many years. I too relaxed with Guy at the helm, it was meant to be.

I leaned my head back against the soft interior and a look at the gold clock told me we had about an hour before we hit the Omni. I must have fallen asleep. I had been very busy trying to make sense of this strange situation. From the beginning, my nerves had sensed something was wrong. Now I know they were right on cue.

I don't know how long I napped, but I awakened by the "ding, ding, ding" of gas being pumped and I witnessed Guy going into the station. He assumed I was still asleep. It was one of those multipurpose rest areas and I was alone for the moment.

A Wrong Turn of the Search for a Signing

Suddenly a part of me wanted to be of some use. It was either that, or I had a sense of my usual foreboding of something being "not right".

The cell-phone was in my hands as I had snoozed off. I absently looked at the entry called "Brown Brs" and hit it on impulse. It had been used frequently by Holly.

Luckily the work day hadn't ended and a cheerful receptionist answered. She passed my call on to an upper office.

"Hi Holly, what's up!" was the assuring male voice I heard at the other end.

"We just spoke."

"When will my check be coming in from the San Francisco office?"

"We just answered that and you know these things take time. The commissions can't be calculated until the whole show is over."

At this time he became almost patronizing. Perhaps he knew of her condition.

Something had been nagging me about the conversation I had been listening to between Guy and the west coast office. Guy's voice just didn't seem natural, it seemed a little fake, or rehearsed. I realized what it was. The pauses were missing that would have normally occurred.

I had been unable to make my call at the time. Now I was convinced that I had been listening to a well practiced one sided conversation.

I was still on the phone with my call to the accountant. Guy had still not returned and Holly's manager was saying, "I thought I told Ellyn you still had quite a few thousand in your Visa account. Use that for now. I'll make adjustments next week if you need more. Talk to Guy, he's making changes to head in a new direction to make your situation more comfortable. I'll have to be going."

"Wait, did my husband just call you?" He hadn't.

I was totally awake now. What was going on? The accountant didn't say anything about a check going to North Charleston. He'd said "These things take a while." Why had Guy lied, and what did I really know about him or about any of this?"

That someone had been blowing smoke all around me and finally into my nose was all I really did know. It hadn't been Holly. She didn't qualify as sound enough. All I really knew about Richard was his complete loyalty to my friend, it never faltered.

That left Guy, and Guy alone who was responsible.

I made a quick calculation of the differences in his strong athletic body and my frail stature. I hadn't exactly been playing tennis all these years as he had.

"Oh, no, here he comes." I jumped out of the car and with a quick "My turn!" and I headed for the cafeteria before he could stop me. It was my age. Women of my age just don't follow directions.

I walked inside hastily and asked if there was a clinic on the premises, I was off of my medication. "Please call 911."

"Move quickly, this has happened before. It never ends well!"

To their credit, they took me seriously and ordered a transport immediately. I knew I'd rather be hospitalized in the south than be in that car with a killer.

In any case, I needed the safety right now of an indifferent EMT team.

I'd much rather have the choice of solving this puzzling case anywhere but on route to Charleston, even if it meant a hospital room. When I explained the danger I was in later on they would understand.

A Wrong Turn of the Search for a Signing

Poor Margaret never had that choice. Guy seemed to pick on women who didn't have the strength to fight back.

CHAPTER FOURTEEN

Inside the Hospital

I was in a small room on the first floor, somewhere in the emergency wing. My fate would be decided by these uniformed figures in white.

It was pretty obvious I had recovered from my mysterious illness. The personnel in these strange flowered jumpsuits showed no interest in me, at last.

My vital signs were all normal, no surprise to me.

My cell-phone barked for the last time, I hoped so at any rate. It was Robert.

I knew I might be in trouble with the authorities for my staged event back in the interstate cafeteria, but I hoped once they knew the facts they would be lenient. I had been in the clutches of a killer, one who as yet hadn't been arrested. I alone knew it to be so.

Robert assured me there was a good chance I was right.

These were the facts as he relayed them to me. Richard was in lockup in the local jail, after resisting arrest pretty violently with the security team. A gun was found in his possession, which added to the strength of an arrest, and additional force was called in.

A Wrong Turn of the Search for a Signing

Holly was not able to defend her old friend, or any one it seemed. She was in need of medical attention, and she was failing quickly. Her confusion was apparent.

The security team talked her into taking her pills, after contacting her physician. The disorientation was taking extreme control of her and attempts were being made had to admit her locally. She was resisting any attempt to "lock her up again".

Robert was still with the local authorities and was filling them in with the facts of Lake George disappearance. No one had accused Richard as no one was aware of the disappearance of Margaret.

I relayed my reason for being hospitalized and assured him I was fine. He believed me.

I just wasn't one to make up stories. Would any one believe him, I just wasn't sure?

Being a minister of some repute has some value, and I knew he would sway them in the long run. At least, it had in the past.

Holly was safe and in good hands. It was all that counted.

One thing was sure, after my latest stunt, my qualification didn't muster up. I wouldn't offer any suggestions for a long time.

"Mom, find a chair, sit in it and don't move! I'll find you."

I did exactly as I was told.

I had a Christmas to celebrate! I didn't know where I'd be spending it, but it would be in my old familiar jeans and graying hair.

The sound of "Jingle Bells" exploded through the gloom from out of nowhere, as I peeked down as my cell. I almost answered it. It turned out to be someone else's. The Christmas joviality had taken over.

Don't these people ever take anything seriously?

CHAPTER SIXTEEN

Back at the Treetops

The parlor of the little B & B was a fresh breath of Christmas. It was one of those turn of the century (not this century) establishments where the beautiful hand carved baby waited until Christmas Eve to be officially installed in His seat of honor.

We were all there, and grateful to be there. Holly, my son and I, and Richard were all celebrating the Happy Noel, along with several other of their faithful guests. There was a Yule Tide punch and, of course, beautifully decorated pastries.

Only Holly seemed not to understand the strain the four of us had been under. Her pretty features were unalterably festive.

I noticed now that she seemed to be seeing someone behind me while she spoke to me. It was very unnerving, but at least I understood it now.

My son was anxious to be home and I couldn't blame him. He was constantly looking at the clock and restlessly talking on his cell-phone, between Holly's doctor and pharmacy. His flight left in the morning. I'll never get him to travel with me again.

Richard was on his way outside to check out the Cadillac limo for the long ride home. I grabbed him as he passed by and asked if he had read Holly's latest novel.

A Wrong Turn of the Search for a Signing

"No", he answered, "She's the best author of the century. I don't have to read it."

He was totally unaware of the questionable authorship of the book he had been chasing around the country. He was just glad to be released by the authorities.

Although the room was the most festive I'd seen, my mood was very somber. Our little group had been through a lot. We couldn't share it with this small crowd. It had nothing to do with Christmas, and they were all pleased to be sharing it with a celebrated author. It was just as well they knew nothing at all about my hospital stay and Holly's illness.

Holly was at this moment signing copies which the owners of the establishment had purchased at the local book store. They had not told anyone in town that HC was staying with them.

As for me, I looked spectacular. I was wearing the Kelly green raw silk with bright red and green strings of beads which I'd purchased earlier in town. They matched the copper streaks in my hair, which had been done at the same time.

"Oh no, here she comes!" Holly was on her way over to see me, and now I had no idea how to handle the situation of her illness.

"You look great. The eyebrows, you've finally had them waxed. Merry Christmas", she said as she presented me with beautiful chunky gold earrings. "Here, put them to good use."

I was so embarrassed! I had forgotten a gift for her. That didn't seem to matter to her at all. In fact, nothing at all seemed to matter!

Just then, a gentleman in a tux approached the baby grand and played "White Christmas".

It was just what I needed at the time. I didn't know why, but I didn't want to be alone with Holly. Our relationship had changed. Her illness was severe, worse than I had been aware of and I didn't know how to proceed. Should I confide in her about the disappearance of Margaret, and Guy's possible involvement?

Of course, that was the problem, and the problem was Guy. No one seemed sure of where he was. He had never shown up at the Omni. He was probably aware that I, at least, was suspicious of his part in the crime.

No one was sure at all where Margaret was as well, and he knew that I had figured out something while in the car with him. He had overlooked the fact that I had tried to use the identical cell-phone and couldn't get through because of the dead zone.

Any calls by Guy had to have been made for my benefit.

In any case, Guy had never shown up at all to rescue his bride-in-distress.

Richard was more of a gopher, and always had been, according to Holly. He was en route to Holly's book-signing with her at the time. He was having the car serviced in Atlantic City at the time of Holly's visit to the church.

Richard, on our return to Treetops, had filled in the missing details of the last known scene of the Lake George estate for us, not in front of Holly, of course.

It seemed Holly had been in Menlo Park just north of Ocean City in a clinic. She was being treated for Parkinson's disease and tests were being performed.

Guy returned to Lake George to tell both him and Margaret about her illness.

At the same time, Richard overheard the news from her publishers on the phone. They were going ahead with the book.

He was sure Holly would welcome the news. He was fond of his employer and headed south to tell her about it. Her

A Wrong Turn of the Search for a Signing

temporary illness hadn't mattered. Her new sleek Cadillac was all that he thought of. It would surely lift her mood.

He left Guy and Margaret alone and headed for Menlo Park. He was right. She was on the phone making plans.

It may have been that Guy all along had known the book he had submitted was written by Margaret. His motive is unclear. He may have been planning to help her submit it and she didn't want his interference. It could also be that the old romantic charm that he had once possessed wasn't working this time.

What is clear is that Margaret was never again seen by anyone. An intensive search would be made of the massive property in Lake George.

Holly, as far as anyone knew, was convinced that her husband had incarcerated her so he could be with her new assistant. She had no intention of seeing him again.

This tragic play was about to make its final curtain.

I caught my reflection in the long mirror beside the piano alongside the softly lighted Christmas tree. I looked at the elegant figure in green. I laughed as I compared it with the pathetic elderly lady in the interstate cafeteria having a meltdown the day before.

This image lacked only one thing, a confident smile that things were going as well as I had planned all along.

I happened to glance away and spotted the look on the face of the pianist. His face was briefly unmasked and I saw for a moment the strangest look. It said, "I've seen it all at these rich folk's parties, people who can't get enough of looking at themselves."

He thought I had a consuming interest in the image presented. This was not what I was doing. I simply didn't recognize this person in the mirror.

Yet, he was right. They couldn't get enough of themselves, these rich folks!

It was Holly who had created this new vision in the mirror, not me. She alone had that creative talent, it was what she did best with her characters, and I owed her a lot. I would make the long ride home with Holly and Richard, and see my old friend safely home. They had both asked me to.

I would have to explain later on to Robert who wanted me on that plane with him.

That would be one of the hardest tasks I'd have to face.

Meanwhile, in the neighborhood of Lake George, it was undisputed that Margaret and Guy were the last two in the area at the time of her disappearance.

CHAPTER SEVENTEEN

Home at last

It was so good to be back in my home in Sea Isle City. My brief encounter with celebrity life has left me cold. My aging furniture that surrounds me seems like old friends now. Perhaps this spring I'll give them a new lift, instead of my eyes. I've heard that this surgery is only temporary. I'm in search of something more lasting at this time of my life.

My wardrobe investment bad been relegated to a closet in my spare upper room. I'll look in on it occasionally. Perhaps I'll smile, perhaps not.

I now know the value of these designer suits, and it scares me. My preference is Sears. I cannot even understand the cost of this wardrobe, let alone the cost of one of these suits with accessories. It would take a mortgage from the bank to purchase the entire grouping in the travel bag it was still in.

All I know is they are still here, and will still be here if Holly wants them back. None of us are sure if she really remembers giving them away.

Holly's disease is Parkinson's. It is so evasive, it is hard to know the amount of destruction and how fast the disease will progress.

I've done a short study on the subject of Parkinson's disease. It's proven very hard to detect because the symptoms vary so much. The disease is based on a combination of heredity and physical experience. Because of Holly's extremely active mental exercises, I can only hope the speed of the deterioration is delayed. I'm sure it will be.

I'm so sorry, my dear friend. We all let you down. I should have followed up with your doctor, despite his lack of concern, or what I thought was lack of interest. Where was my natural stubborn streak? I'm afraid it was more interested in sight seeing and foolish fantasies.

What can I say about Guy? He saw your illness as a chance to jump ship. He came really close to a complete getaway, no thanks to me.

Holly is back in the facility at Menlo Park, and under the best care she can possibly get.

It is only now that I understand the tremors, uncertainty and looks of fear that overcame Holly toward the end of our trip. It happened more often than I thought at the time.

Far more often!

What would happen next to our dear friend? We have a new association for the old sorority who had been merely friends before this. Now we have a genuine concern for Holly. All of us agree on her choice of Richard for her power of attorney.

Once again her instincts were far better than mine. I should have recognized that a relationship that went back over thirty years told its own story of mutual trust.

Richard has taken a new apartment in Menlo Park. He's got a big job ahead of him!

A search is still being done to find any trace of an heir for the proceeds of Margaret's successful novel. Guy had done a thorough job of selecting a replacement for Richard. Luckily a record had been found of the applicants in a journal among Guy's possessions. The notes inserted in the borders will

A Wrong Turn of the Search for a Signing

help prove premeditation. He preferred applicants with few associates.

Poor Guy, he hadn't been involved in enough crimes in his lifetime, or he would have cleaned out his room a little better. His wife had been the expert at crime detection. His only experience had been in spending her fortune.

The Brown accounting firm turned over evidence showing his withdrawals of investments made this past year. Deposits were made into offshore accounts as he made plans to leave the country. He had come dangerously close to hiding this crime and moving on with his life.

It is still undisputed that Margaret and Guy were the last two in the area at the time of her disappearance. Interrogated staff testified to this fact. Guy is in custody at this time.

An entire team from the Lake George area had volunteered to search the entire area. The residents had loved their local celebrity. She was known for her generous donations to the charity regattas and always let them use her lakeside grounds whenever asked.

The story was well known of Margaret's disappearance and spread quickly.

Everyone knew it was a case of spiritual possession, no question!

"We've never trusted him, never had a reason to!"

Guy has been still not been found guilty of the horrendous crime of Margaret's murder. Her body had still not been found yet.

The team is determined to find Margaret, and they are now working around the boathouse and under it. I believe they are closer than ever to a successful conclusion to this horrendous crime.

As for me, Angellica, I have a lot of reading to do. I'm still Holly's biggest fan and will be for a long time. When I visit Holly, we'll have a lot to talk about.

Maybe I'll find that perfect spot to write the great American Novel. I prefer to stay home and write about it.

Yet I never did get to see the waterfront in Savannah. They say it's the best feature of all!

Where did I put Sam's card?

www.ingramcontent.com/pod-product-compliance
Lightning Source LLC
LaVergne TN
LVHW040200080526
838202LV00042B/3249